Miss Kitty and the Krackerknocker

Written by
Michael Gerhardt

Illustrated by
Charlotte Wismer

Published in the United States by TBB Publishing

Text and illustrations copyrighted 2019 by TBB Publishing

ISBN: 9781091267534

This book is dedicated to Lola W. Gerhardt, my mother and Charlotte's Great Grandmother. She taught me to not just read the words in a book, but to try to understand the ideas, concepts and feelings the author was trying to convey. She has also enthusiastically supported Charlotte in all of her extraordinary creative endeavors in music and art. Thank you Lola, for everything.

Nana Anna was a very small person who lived in a very small house that sat in a very small meadow by the Great North Sea. Next to her very small house was a very small sandy road that led to a very small village where, once a month, they held a very small market, where Nana Anna sold wool yarn she spun and dyed herself.

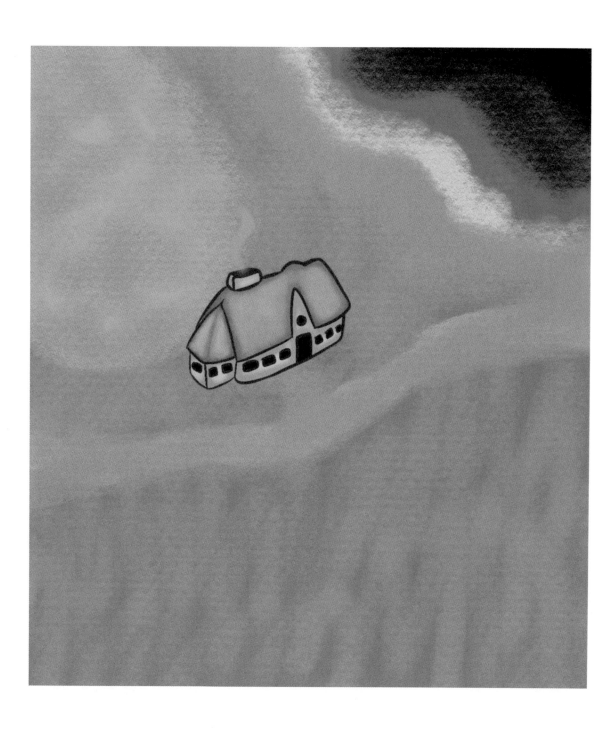

Nana Anna lived alone, unless you counted Miss Kitty, a very small ball of grey fur that looked like one of Nana Anna's balls of wool, except smaller, and with very large blue eyes. Nana Anna didn't see Miss Kitty very often, because Miss Kitty was not only very small, she was afraid of EVERYTHING. Miss Kitty was very afraid of thunder, enormously afraid of lightning and driving rain, and deathly afraid of loud noises, the dark, any animal bigger than she was, things that go bump in the night, and even her own shadow.

One night there was a terrible storm that blew in from the Great North Sea. The wind shook the windows of the very small house, the lightning lit up the very small field, and the rain pounded the roof for hours. Miss Kitty disappeared and Nana Anna didn't see her for the rest of the night.

The next morning Nana Anna went walking along the shore of the Great North Sea, where she spotted a large, dark lump on the sand. She approached it cautiously, because she had never seen anything like it before. And when she got close to it, the shape moved. Nana Anna jumped back, not sure what to do.

The odd shape made a noise that sounded like a groan and rolled over. It was an animal of some kind, and Nana Anna stepped closer for a better look. The body was bigger than some small horses and it was lumpy, and covered with fur in some places, feathers in others, scales in still others, and even some small armor plates in other places.

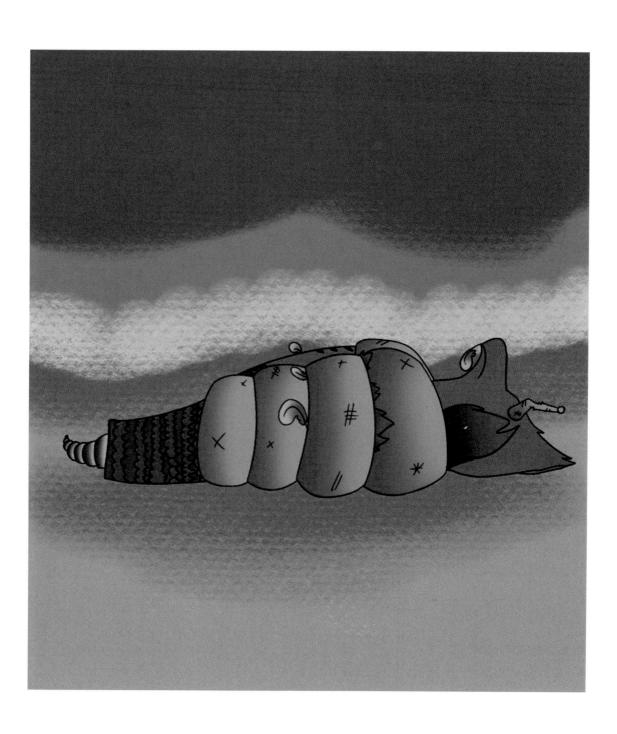

Nana Anna picked up a stick and poked the animal's body gently. It grunted and got to its feet, all six of them, and Nana Anna got a good look at the animal's head for the first time. It was very large, and oddly shaped, with deep set brown and yellow eyes, a large pointy nose, a mouth full of yellow, very pointy teeth and a big round horn in the middle of its forehead. It was not a very pretty animal, thought Nana Anna, and that made her a little sad.

"Hello, big one," she said softly, putting her hand on its nose. The animal grunted and turned away from Nana Anna and walked off down the beach. Nana Anna watched it until it disappeared into the woods.

The next day Farmer Owen brought eggs and milk to Nana Anna. After she thanked Farmer Owen, paid him and put the eggs and milk away, they chatted a bit. Nana Anna told him about the strange animal on the beach.

"A Krackerknocker," he said.

"A what?"

"A Krackerknocker."

"What's a Krackerknocker," she asked.

"What you saw," he replied.

"Oh. How do you know?"

"My grandfather saw one once and told us children all about it," Farmer Owen said.

"Must be why the chickens have been so nervous."

"Oh, dear," Nana Anna said. "Do Krackerknockers eat chickens?"

"Krackerknockers eat everything. Best lock your door when I leave," Farmer Owen said.

They chatted a little more and then said goodbye. Nana Anna closed the door and locked it, and then looked around the very small room. Miss Kitty was nowhere to be seen, and Nana Anna worried just a little.

The very next night, Nana Anna was sitting at her spinning wheel finishing up the last string of yarn for market day the next morning when there was a very loud bang at the door. She looked up, startled, and stopped spinning. After a few seconds there was another bang at the door, louder than the first one, and the door shuddered and shook.

"Oh, dear," Nana Anna said to herself. *What should I do?* She wondered. And then there was a third big bang and the door flew open and a big, ugly animal trudged in on six legs and stopped in the middle of her very small room and glared at her with its ugly green eyes. It was the Krackerknocker.

The Krackerknocker looked around the room and then began to eat. First he ate the very small stack of firewood by the fireplace. Then he ate a very small chair sitting at the very small table in the corner, then he ate the second chair, and then he ate the table. And Nana Anna still sat quite still.

But, when the Krackerknocker went to the corner and began eating her market basket and the balls of wool yarn inside the basket, Nana Anna had had enough. She jumped up from her spinning wheel and shouted.

"You stop that right now!"

The Krackerknocker ignored her and kept on eating the wool.

Nana Anna picked up the iron poker at the fireplace and stepped across the room to stand right behind the Krackerknocker.

"Stop it, now, I said," she spoke in her firmest tone, then took a deep breath and slapped the Krackerknocker on its behind with the poker. The Krackerknocker stopped eating and turned around and growled at her. It was an ugly growl and it showed his long, yellow teeth, most of them with pieces of yarn stuck between them.

Nana Anna shook the iron poker at the Krackerknocker.

"I want you to leave right now", she said. But the Krackerknocker grabbed the poker out of Nana Anna's hand with its mouth and ate it in two bites. His eyes glared at Nana Anna and she glared right back.

"Now, out!" Nana said, but the Krackerknocker shook his head, and butted her hard in the chest with the horn in the middle of his forehead. She staggered backward and fell right onto her very small bed. The Krackerknocker took a step forward and began eating the bedsheets at her feet. Nana Anna was finally afraid.

Suddenly Miss Kitty appeared at the edge of the bed, climbed up the side and put herself right between the Krackerknocker and Nana Anna.

The Krackerknocker stopped chewing, studied Miss Kitty, and then opened its mouth so it could eat Missy Kitty. But Miss Kitty took a very small step backward, took a deep breath, and shouted at the Krackerknocker.

"Meow!" she said and the Krackerknocker stopped and blinked. Then it opened its mouth wider and shouted back at Miss Kitty.

"**GROWL!**"

Miss Kitty tumbled over backward and ended up sitting on Nana Anna's chest. The Krackerknocker opened his mouth again to take a bite of Nana Anna's foot, and Miss Kitty took a deeper breath and shouted.

"**MEOW!**" she said, but the Krackerknocker just kept coming.

Finally, Miss Kitty took the biggest breath she had ever taken in her entire life and shouted at the Krackerknocker. And this time her shout turned into a roar.

"RRRROOOOAAAARRRR!!!"

The Krackerknocker stopped and shook its head, trying to get the terrible sound out of its ears. But Missy Kitty kept roaring.

"RRRROOOOAAAARRRR!!!!"

And the very small windows began to shake, but still Missy Kitty kept roaring.

"RRRROOOOAAAARRRR!!!!"

And the very small house itself began to shake, and the Krackerknocker too.

And Missy Kitty kept roaring.

"RRRROOOOAAAARRRR!!!!"

The Krackerknocker's eyes began to show a little panic as its body began to shake more violently. It was the longest, loudest roar he had ever heard. And Miss Kitty still roared on.

"RRRROOOOAAAARRRR!!!!"

And the very small windows blew out of their very small frames, and the Krackerknocker shook even more. It shook so badly Miss Kitty almost couldn't tell what it was anymore.

But she continued to roar.

"RRRROOOOAAAARRRR!!!!"

And suddenly the Krackerknocker exploded into a million small flakes that floated out the windows and disappeared into the night. Miss Kitty stopped roaring and the very small room was suddenly very quiet.

Miss Kitty turned and studied Nana Anna, who looked like she was asleep. Miss Kitty climbed up and licked her face until she woke up.

Nana Anna sat up and looked around the very small room. The firewood was gone, and so were the two chairs, the table, the windows, most of the bed clothes, and, best of all so was the Krackerknocker.

But there, in the very small corner, was the market basket, and it was magically filled with the balls of yarn Nana Anna had worked so hard to produce.

Nana Anna picked up Miss Kitty and peered at her face. Something seemed a little different. Something pleasant had appeared on Missy Kitty's face. Nana Anna thought it must be confidence. She smiled and patted Miss Kitty on the head.

"Thank you, Miss Kitty," she said, and Miss Kitty just purred a very small purr in return, and she was never afraid of anything ever again.

THE END

YOUR TURN!

What do you think the Krackerknocker looks like?

You can draw it right here!

Name: _____

Date: _____

Share your drawing on social media using
#krackerknocker

YOUR TURN!

What do you think the Krackerknocker looks like?

You can draw it right here!

Name: _____

Date: _____

Share your drawing on social media using
#krackerknocker

MICHAEL GERHARDT

Mr. Gerhardt is an award-winning author of twenty novels. *Miss Kitty and the Krackerknocker* is his first Children's Book. He has also written a Young Adult book, *The Incredible Cousins and the Magic Caboose*, a fantasy written with, and about, his six grandchildren. Mr. Gerhardt lives near Philadelphia and continues to write.

Visit megerhardt.com to learn more about Mr. Gerhardt's books.

CHARLOTTE WISMER

Ms. Wismer is the talented artist who illustrated *Miss Kitty and the Krackerknocker* when she was thirteen years old. She was twelve when she collaborated with Mr. Gerhardt, her grandfather on *The Incredible Cousins and the Magic Caboose*. She currently attends high school and enjoys art, music and reading. Visit charlottewismer.com to view more of Charlotte's work.

Made in the
USA
Middletown, DE